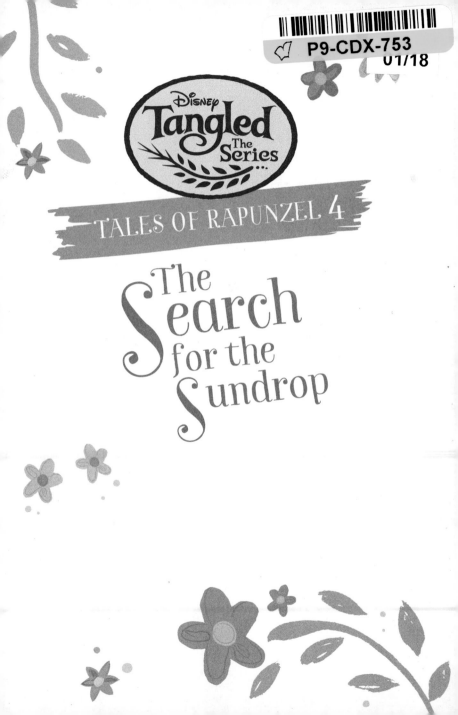

Disney
Tangled
The Series

TALES OF RAPUNZEL 4

The Search for the Sundrop

For Lauren
—K.M.

rhcbooks.com

ISBN 978-0-7364-3764-6 (trade) —
ISBN 978-0-7364-9019-1 (lib. bdg.)

Printed in the United States of America

10 9 8 7 6 5 4 3 2 1

DISNEY
Tangled
The Series

TALES OF RAPUNZEL 4

The
Search
for the
Sundrop

Adapted by
Kathy McCullough

Illustrated by
Arianna Rea

Random House 🏠 New York

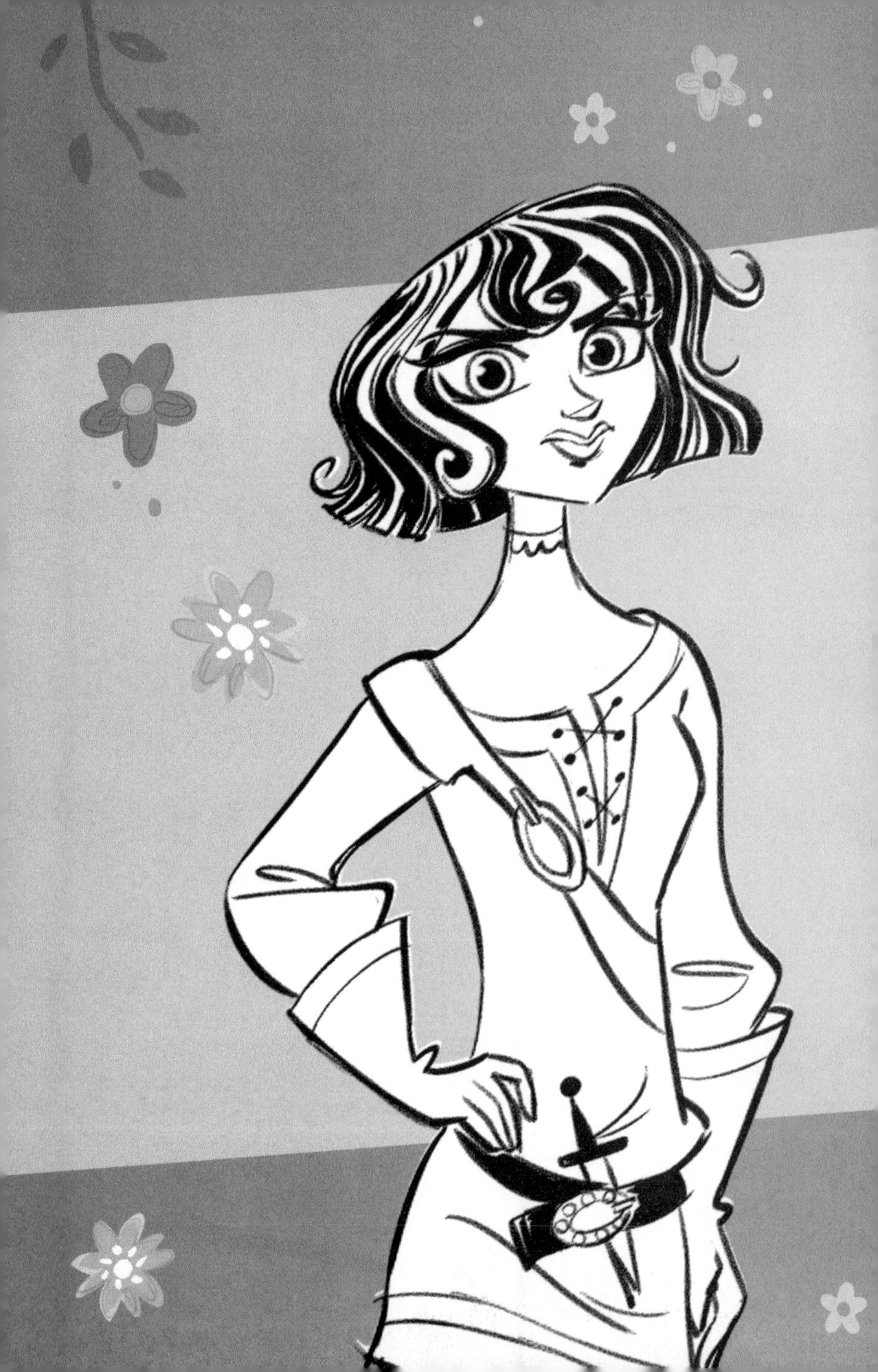

Tale One

The
Quest
for
Varian

CHAPTER 1

Rapunzel giggled as her father struggled to free himself from a tangle of long purple streamers. "It's not funny!" King Frederic protested. "Have you any idea how difficult—"

Rapunzel lifted up her equally long blond braid before he could finish. She was very familiar with being tangled. Just combing her hair out every morning—before braiding it—took almost an hour!

The king laughed and they shared a smile as Rapunzel freed him from the streamers. She had been surprised when her father offered to help her

1

decorate the castle courtyard for her nineteenth birthday celebration in a few days. He was usually so serious. It was nice to joke around with him and have fun for once.

Rapunzel and the king finished hanging the streamers and brought out the kites that would line the courtyard. The kites resembled the flying lanterns King Frederic and Queen Arianna had launched every year on Rapunzel's birthday, after she'd been kidnapped as a baby by an evil woman named Mother Gothel.

Growing up, Rapunzel had seen the lanterns from the window of the tower where Mother Gothel had imprisoned her. She would watch the glowing lanterns float through the night sky, wondering what they meant—unaware

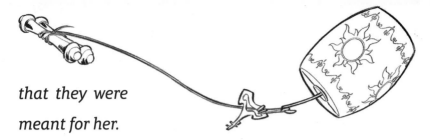

that they were
meant for her.

Most of the kites were simply colored gold, but Rapunzel spotted one with decorative borders. A key was attached to the string. And below that, a scroll. Rapunzel watched as a breeze caused it to float away.

A moment later, Rapunzel was no longer in the courtyard of Corona. Instead, she was in Old Corona, a village a few miles away where her

friend Varian lived. The sun was gone, and clouds blanketed the sky. Spiky black rocks stuck up from the ground throughout the village.

More rocks burst up around her. Rapunzel stared in shock as her hair began to glow.

"Rapunzel!" a high-pitched voice called. It sounded like Varian.

Rapunzel looked around, searching for her friend. She saw her father standing a few yards away . . . yet somehow still in sunny Corona. She moved toward him—but a wall of rocks shot up, separating them.

A hand grabbed her arm, and she spun around to find Varian beside her. "Help me!" he cried. "You promised!"

But before she could respond, more rocks rose from the earth and surrounded him. There was an explosion of light, and Rapunzel's glowing hair whirled up around her. . . .

Rapunzel snapped open her eyes, freeing herself from her nightmare to find she was no longer in bed. She was hanging in midair, suspended above her

balcony. Strands of her glowing hair fanned out around her like the legs of a spider and clung to the stones of the castle's wall. The glow faded and the strands broke loose from the stones.

Rapunzel fell. . . .

"Rapunzel!" cried Eugene, Rapunzel's boyfriend, as he rushed into the room. He reached the balcony and caught her just in time. "What happened?"

Rapunzel looked up at him, dazed and frightened. "I . . . I don't know." Eugene set her down and she hugged him tightly, trying to force away her fear.

She had dreamed about the black rocks before. Each time, they seemed to be coming after her—just as they had in real life

when she'd first seen them, on a cliff outside the kingdom.

The rocks alone were menacing, but now it seemed that even the dreams themselves were dangerous. . . .

In her art studio later that morning, Rapunzel painted the images she remembered from her dream, trying to make sense of them. Pascal, her pet chameleon, sat on her shoulder, watching her fill her latest canvas with thick slashes of black, each one rising to a sharp point.

Eugene and Cassandra, Rapunzel's lady-in-waiting, studied the finished paintings. One portrayed the lanterns soaring off into the sky; another showed Rapunzel's blond hair flying around her head.

Rapunzel knew her dreams were trying to tell her something. "The rocks, my hair, Varian . . . it's as if they're all connected," she told her friends. "I have to find out *how*."

Rapunzel first met Varian when she'd asked for his help to figure out why her long hair had returned. Varian was an alchemist, with a laboratory filled with potions he'd invented and machines he'd built to test the properties of all sorts of things. Yet he hadn't been able to solve the mystery of her hair.

"What if the dream was a warning?" Eugene asked. "Telling you to stay here, where you're safe?"

She knew Eugene might be right. But if the rocks *were* dangerous, it wasn't only Rapunzel who was in danger.

Shortly after her first visit to Varian, a cluster of black rocks had sprouted up behind his house. Varian had come to the castle not long ago to tell her that more rocks had appeared. She had promised to help him, but a terrible blizzard had hit the kingdom, and she'd been too busy dealing with the storm to keep her promise.

But what if the rocks had destroyed Varian's house in the meantime? What if they had spread through his whole village, as they had in her dream?

Rapunzel remembered another key part of her dream—her father. She needed answers, and if anyone could tell her what was really going on in the kingdom, *he* could.

CHAPTER 2

In the past, whenever Rapunzel had asked her father about the rocks, he'd refused to talk about them. But she couldn't let him brush off her questions any longer. It was clear she was connected to the rocks in some way—maybe even responsible for them. She needed to know the truth.

Rapunzel found King Frederic in the throne room, talking to one of his advisors. The king's expression was grim—the opposite of the sunny, smiling face he'd had in her dream.

Rapunzel hurried up to him. "Dad, the

11

black rocks . . . I'm worried they've—"

The king raised his hand. "I thought I made it clear we were not going to discuss this."

"I'm worried Varian is in danger," insisted Rapunzel. "Has anyone been to Old Corona lately?"

King Frederic realized his daughter wouldn't give up until he gave her an answer. He led her over to a miniature model of the kingdom. Dozens of tiny flags had been pinned in different locations—most of them in Old Corona.

"I've been aware of the rocks for some time," the king told her. "They posed a real problem: destroying homes, damaging roads. . . ." He plucked out the flags one by one. "Fortunately, we've taken care of them. The rocks have been

removed, and the people of Old Corona are all fine."

Rapunzel sighed in relief. Old Corona was safe. "Thanks for being honest with me," she told her father.

The king guided Rapunzel to the door. "Now run along," he said with a smile, looking happy again. "You've got more pressing issues—like planning your birthday party!"

Rapunzel hugged her father and hurried off to tell Cassandra and Eugene the good news.

She found her friends in the courtyard, which had been decorated for her birthday, just as in her dream. A gentle wind fluttered the purple streamers, and a single kite sailed into the courtyard and headed toward her statue. It was the kite from her dream!

The kite, weighed down by an iron key dangling from its string, floated toward her. Below the key was a note. Rapunzel read it.

Rapunzel,

I need your help, now more than ever. I may have discovered the key to the rocks. Find the bronze cylinder in my lab. But be careful. They're watching, and they'll do anything to stop you.

—Varian

"Who's 'they'?" asked Cassandra.

Rapunzel didn't know. What she *did* know

was that Varian still needed her help. King Frederic might have taken care of the rocks, but there was obviously more to the story than he'd told her. She needed to find out the *whole* truth.

Rapunzel turned to her friends. "We have to go to Old Corona."

There was only one horse Rapunzel trusted to take them: Maximus. Max was the top horse in the royal guard and Rapunzel's friend. He'd come to her rescue more than once, and he could be trusted to keep their trip a secret.

With Max pulling the cart, Rapunzel, Eugene, and Cassandra were soon on the road. Pascal sat on Rapunzel's shoulder, and Owl perched on Cassandra's. Owl was more of a guide than

a pet. When Rapunzel and Cassandra had ventured out to the rocks for the first time, Owl had helped lead the way.

Cassandra, who'd been raised by the captain of the royal guard, wore her guard-in-training uniform, complete with sword. Rapunzel had brought along her own favorite weapon: a frying pan. She hoped she wouldn't have to use it, but Varian *had* warned her someone might try to stop them from finding the cylinder.

They passed through a small forest, and when they emerged, Rapunzel spotted a spiky black rock poking up from the middle of a nearby field. She stared at it in surprise. "My dad told me all the black rocks had been removed," she said.

Eugene shrugged. "So they missed one."

"Um, guys . . ." Cassandra pointed ahead. In the distance, dozens of rocks dotted the land.

"Looks more like they missed closer to one *hundred*," said Eugene.

"Do you think your father lied?" Cassandra asked Rapunzel.

"Of course not," Rapunzel said quickly. Her father would never lie to her. "But he clearly has no idea how bad things have gotten out here." The king either didn't know how many rocks there really were, or more rocks had sprouted up to replace the ones he'd removed.

As they drew closer to Old Corona, the clusters of rocks grew denser, poking up through ruined houses and ravaged pastures. "I've never seen anything like it," said Cassandra.

Rapunzel had, though. In her dream.

They made their way toward Varian's house, which was on the far side of town, near the outer wall of the kingdom. Soon there were so many rocks, the road was blocked completely and Max was forced to stop. There were narrow openings between some of

the rocks, but it was impossible to know which path led to Varian's. Rapunzel hopped off the cart and approached the rocks.

"Remember what happens when you touch them," warned Cassandra. She nodded to Rapunzel's braid, which was glowing. The last time Rapunzel had come in contact with the rocks, there had been a giant explosion and Rapunzel's blonde hair returned.

"I'll just have to be careful," said Rapunzel.

"We need a bird's-eye view," said Cassandra. She called out to Owl, who flew off, disappearing over the forest of rocks. A few seconds later, he reappeared, waving his wing in the direction they should go.

Rapunzel instructed Max to stand guard. With Pascal clinging to her shoulder, Rapunzel made her way into the narrow opening Owl had indicated, followed by Eugene and Cassandra. The rocks cut off the sunlight, but Rapunzel's glowing hair lit the way.

They emerged in front of Varian's house

and ventured inside to find his laboratory ravaged by rocks. Broken bottles and pieces of machinery littered the floor. "Someone should explain to this kid the importance of an organized, clutter-free workspace," commented Eugene.

As they searched through the rubble, Rapunzel tried to imagine where Varian might have hidden the cylinder. Her gaze landed on a large red book on Varian's desk. It looked important—and mysterious. She hurried over and opened it, revealing a secret compartment.

Nestled in the compartment was a small bronze tube. "I found it!" declared Rapunzel, holding up the cylinder.

"Great!" Eugene said. "Now let's get out of here. This place is giving me the creeps."

As Rapunzel crossed the room, she passed a large object covered by a tarp. There was a gap in the cover, and a gleaming eye peered out at her.

Startled but curious, she pulled back the tarp to reveal Quirin, Varian's father, frozen in a giant block of amber.

Behind him, also trapped in the amber, was a spiky black rock. . . .

CHAPTER 3

Rapunzel shivered in horror as she stared up at Quirin. Here was genuine proof that the rocks were a danger to others, not just her.

Suddenly, the laboratory door slammed open, and a masked figure stormed toward them. He was dressed all in black and held a halberd—a long pole with an axe-shaped blade at the end. "Hand over the flask!" the figure demanded.

Cassandra drew out her sword, but the masked man whacked it with his halberd, causing her to stumble backward into the wall.

"You crossed the line, bub," said Eugene, grabbing the halberd. The masked man roughly shoved him away. Eugene crashed into the wall, collapsing next to Cassandra. "Hoo boy," he gasped. "*That* was a mistake."

Rapunzel had left her frying pan in the cart, but she snatched up one of Varian's potions from his lab table. "Stay back," she warned the figure. "I've got a table full of alchemy and I'm not afraid to use it!" She hurled the bottle, which smashed to the floor, sending up a smokescreen.

The masked man coughed and waved away the smoke—but he continued to close in.

Pascal handed more bottles to Rapunzel, who threw them at the intruder. Soon, the table was empty—except for a large purple crystal.

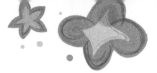

Rapunzel recognized it as the glue potion she and Cassandra had gotten stuck in when they'd first visited Varian's lab.

Rapunzel flung the crystal at the figure's feet. It burst, covering the floor—and the masked man's boots—in a sticky purple goo. "That ought to hold you," she said with a grin.

Rapunzel grabbed the bronze cylinder, and she and her friends raced outside and back into the forest of rocks. As before, Rapunzel's glowing hair lit the way through the narrow path.

The masked figure suddenly appeared in front of them, blocking their way. Rapunzel was stunned. How had he gotten free so quickly? They turned to head down another path—but the man again leaped out at them.

Eugene blinked in amazement. "How fast *is* this guy?" he said. They ducked down a different path, and this time, the man didn't appear. They emerged in a wide, unfamiliar field that was covered with rocks. Rapunzel realized they were lost.

A moment later, dozens of masked men in black stepped out from behind the rocks.

"Well, that explains it," said Eugene.

Suddenly, a fierce neigh sounded from behind a rock. Max charged out, a frying pan clutched in his teeth. He barreled through the men, swinging the pan left and right, knocking them down one by one.

"Max!" cried Rapunzel. "You couldn't have come at a better time!" He neighed again and raced over to her. She jumped onto his back, followed by Cassandra and Eugene. They galloped off, leaving the mysterious men behind.

"Those guys want whatever is in this pretty bad," Rapunzel said, holding up the cylinder. "Something tells me we won't make it back to the castle."

Eugene nodded. It was only a matter of time before the masked men were after them again.

"We need somewhere to hide so we can come up with a plan," he said.

Rapunzel spotted a familiar hill in the distance. "I know just the place."

When they reached the hill, Rapunzel pulled on Max's reins. "We're here," she announced.

"*Here?*" Eugene glanced around in confusion. "Where's *here?*"

Rapunzel hopped off Max and led them into a cavelike opening in the hill. The cave turned out to be a tunnel, with a vine-covered opening at the opposite end.

"I'm surprised you don't recognize it," Rapunzel told Eugene. She drew aside the curtain of green vines but was shocked by what she saw. "Actually, I'm not sure *I* recognize it now, either."

Ahead was the tower where Rapunzel had spent her childhood. She'd been back once, when

she'd followed Pascal there after he'd run away. At that time, the tower was still surrounded by a pretty green meadow.

Now it was surrounded by spiky black rocks.

Luckily, the rocks hadn't blocked the opening at the rear of the tower. Rapunzel led her friends up the stone staircase, to the large, round room at the top of the tower that had once been her home.

Eugene guided Max and Owl around the room, pointing out the highlights. "This is where Rapunzel hit me with the frying pan for the first time," he said, gesturing to a spot near a tall wooden wardrobe. Eugene had been a thief then, and he'd climbed through the tower window to hide.

"And that's where I cut her hair to free her from Mother Gothel," he continued, pointing to a long lock of hair on the floor. The ancient Gothel had stayed young by using the magic healing power of Rapunzel's hair. Once Rapunzel's hair was cut, the magic was gone, and Gothel had tumbled out the window, turning to dust as she fell.

Cassandra gazed around the room in awe and tried to imagine being cooped up in one room for years. It must've been horrible! But she noticed Rapunzel had made the room cheerful by covering the walls with lively paintings.

Next to Cassandra, Rapunzel and Pascal sat at the table, studying the cylinder. Rapunzel

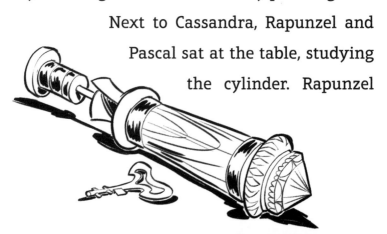

noticed a slit the width of a coin on one end. She held the cylinder up to the skylight and peered into the opening, but she couldn't see anything.

Cassandra plucked the cylinder from Rapunzel's hands and tried to twist off the ends, but they wouldn't budge.

A thought occurred to Rapunzel. "The key!" she cried, reaching into her pocket for the key that had accompanied Varian's note.

When she inserted the key into the cylinder's opening, the cap came off, revealing a rolled-up piece of parchment. "It looks like a scroll," she said.

Meanwhile, Eugene had guided Owl and Max to the tower window. When he glanced

down, his eyes widened with alarm. "Guys! We have a problem!" he yelled.

Rapunzel rushed to the window. The sun had begun to set, but there was still enough light to see the army of masked men scaling the side of the tower.

She glared down at them and declared, "These guys just ticked off the wrong princess!" She was tired of running and hiding. It was time to fight back.

Eugene grinned. "That's my girl," he said, holding out the frying pan.

Rapunzel shook her head. "Frying pans are great—but it's time for an upgrade." She unclipped the barrette at the bottom of her braid.

"What are you doing?" asked Cassandra.

"Letting down my hair," replied Rapunzel,

shaking out her braid and tossing her hair out the window. It soared past the men, to the rocks at the base of the tower. When it hit the rocks, it sent up sizzling sparks, followed by an enormous explosion.

Shock waves shook the tower. The masked men lost their grip on the stones and plunged to the ground.

The building continued to shake. Dust and debris dropped from the tower ceiling. Rapunzel had bought them time by taking care of the masked men, but she and the others needed to get out of the tower—*now.*

CHAPTER 4

Rapunzel and her friends hurried to the stairs leading down through the tower—but the black rocks had broken through the walls, blocking their way.

"I didn't expect them to follow me way up here!" cried Rapunzel. The friends returned to the tower room, but the rocks now blocked the window and pierced the sides of the tower, causing cracks to zigzag up the walls.

Just then, Rapunzel remembered the skylight. "That's the only way out," she said, pointing to the circle of twilight high above them.

Cylinder in hand, she led the others up the steps. They reached the skylight, and one by one they climbed through to the roof.

On the roof, Rapunzel and her friends struggled to keep their balance as the rocks continued their attack on the tower walls. There was no safe way down—but it wasn't safe to stay on the roof, either.

Rapunzel's hair swirled around her as the tower swayed. It gave her an idea. . . .

She explained her plan to the others. "I know it's crazy," she said, "but you're going to have to trust me."

Eugene realized they had no other choice. "Let's go for it," he said, taking her hand.

Cassandra nodded, grabbing Eugene's other hand and wrapping her free arm around Max's neck. Pascal and Owl clung to Max's back.

"Let's go!" cried Rapunzel. They raced to the edge of the roof and took a flying leap.

"I can't believe we're doing this!" shouted Eugene as they plummeted toward the ground.

Rapunzel's hair began to glow. It poufed out, forming a protective sphere around them. As the rocks tore the tower apart, Rapunzel and the others landed safely several feet away.

Rapunzel's hair floated back down around her shoulders. A moment later, the tower collapsed. Once the dust cleared, the moon shone down on a forest of spiky black rocks.

Rapunzel picked up a chunk of stone lying at her feet. It was a fragment from one of the paintings she'd made years before. She shivered, disturbed by the sight. She was grateful to have her freedom and family back, but the destruction of the tower—a big part of her childhood—made her sad.

"Are you okay?" Eugene asked. Rapunzel nodded and dropped the chunk of painting. That time of her life was gone forever.

"Guys!" Cassandra called. She stood a few feet away, pointing to a man lying facedown in the dirt. Other masked figures surrounded him.

Rapunzel marched toward the man. His mask had been knocked off, and when he reached for it, she snatched it out of his hands. "Time for answers," she said.

The man lifted his head—it was

the captain of the guard! Cassandra gasped.
"Dad?"

The captain stood, avoiding his daughter's
eyes. "We had orders to recover the scroll,"

he told Rapunzel. "To keep it from you."

The other figures stood and pulled off their masks—revealing several more royal guards.

"Who?" Rapunzel demanded. *"Who* ordered you?"

The captain hesitated.

"Answer her," said Cassandra.

The captain sighed and lowered his head. "Your father," he told Rapunzel.

Rapunzel couldn't believe it. Her father, the king, a man she trusted more than anyone in Corona, had lied to her. Not only that, he'd sent men after her to stop her from finding out the truth.

They *hadn't* stopped her, though. She had the scroll.

Cassandra and Eugene closed in around Rapunzel protectively as she unrolled the

parchment. There were no words on it, just symbols of the sun and the moon, and images of pointy black shards.

Rapunzel had no clue what any of it meant.

"Why would your father want to keep this from you?" asked Eugene.

"I don't know," said Rapunzel. "But I'm going to find out."

The End

Tale Two

The
Alchemist
Returns

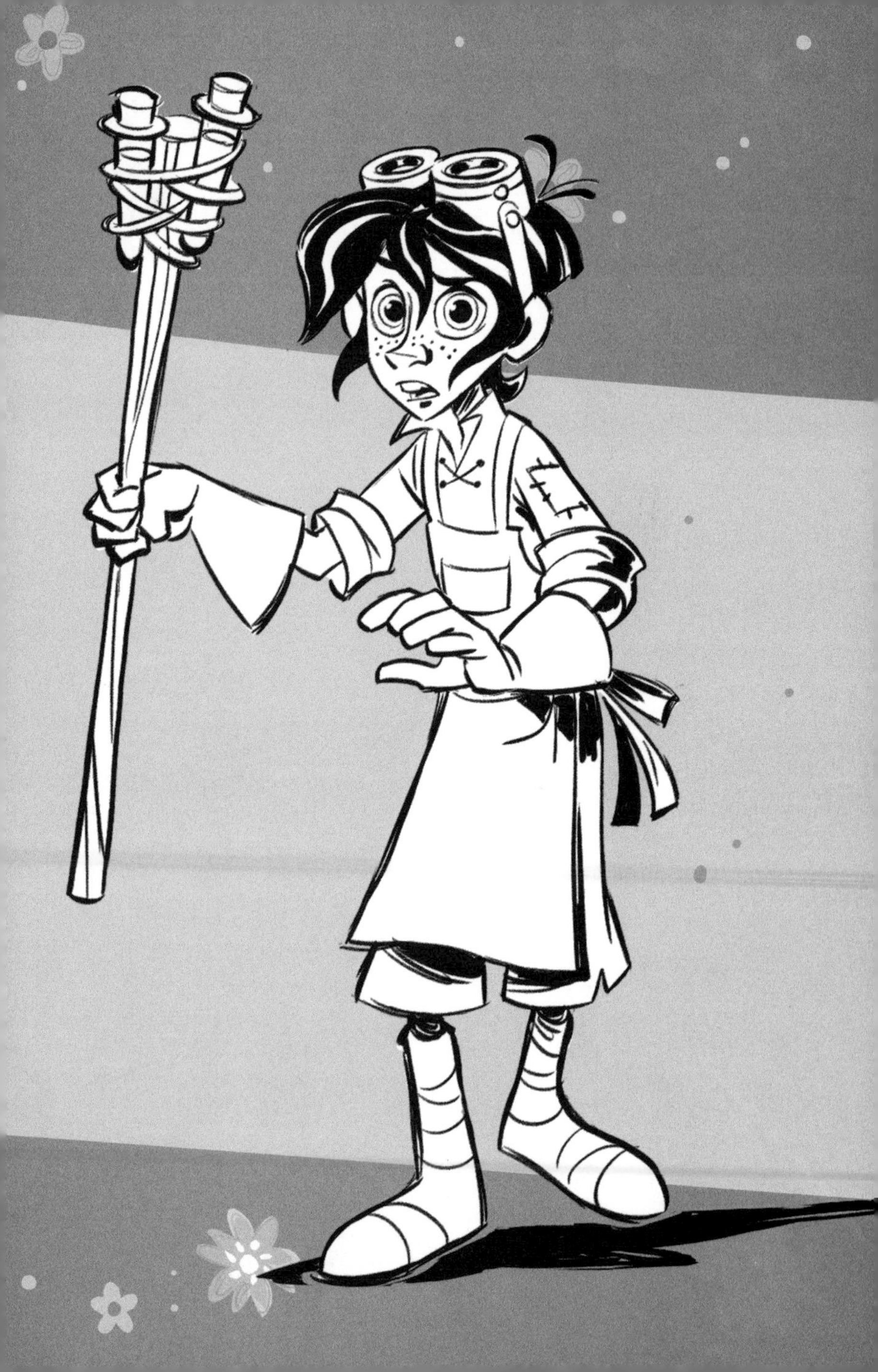

CHAPTER 1

Rapunzel stormed down the castle hallway, her fists clenched. She'd returned to the castle with Eugene and Cassandra at dawn, and although she'd been up all night, she was wide awake.

She found her father in the throne room, speaking with several of his advisors. "You lied to me," she said as she marched up to him.

King Frederic nodded to his advisors, and they scurried past the princess toward the door. "I only wanted to protect you," the king told Rapunzel when they had gone.

"From *what*?" she demanded. "Your own men?" Rapunzel flung her arms wide in frustration. "I want to know why you've been covering up the fact that our kingdom is being destroyed by those black rocks." She met her father's eyes, pleading with him to be honest. "What are you trying to hide?"

The king shook his head. "I'm sorry, my dear. I didn't want to lie to you . . . but you're not ready for the truth."

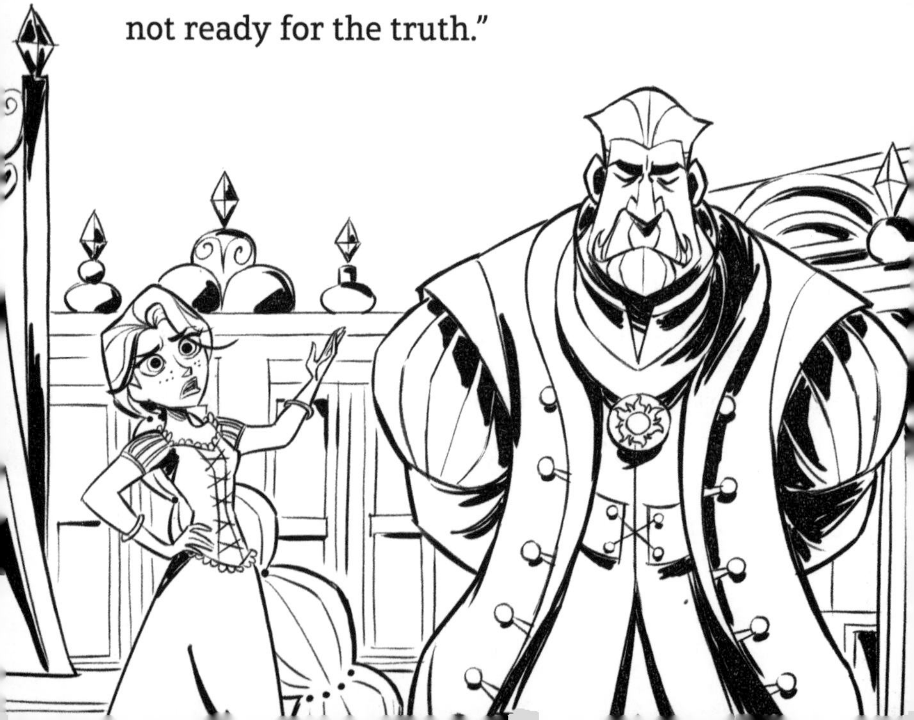

Rapunzel frowned, exasperated. "We're beyond what I am or am not ready for, Dad! People are in danger!"

The king squared his shoulders. "I have the situation under control," he said firmly.

"You're not the first person to lie to me and tell me I'm not ready for the real world." Mother Gothel had also kept Rapunzel in the dark—and had made her feel helpless as a result.

But Rapunzel had changed. She wasn't going to let *anyone* keep the truth from her again. Without waiting for the king's reply, she stormed out, her hands clenched.

It was clear her father wasn't going to tell her anything. She would have to find the answers herself—before it was too late.

* * *

Eugene leaned against a wall in Rapunzel's studio, watching her pace. Pascal scurried back and forth along the windowsill, trying to keep up with her and mimicking her grim expression.

"I'm guessing Corona won't be hosting a father-daughter dance anytime soon," observed Eugene, hoping a joke might lighten the mood. Rapunzel had told him about her conversation with the king.

Rapunzel and Pascal stopped pacing and glared at him. Eugene shrugged sheepishly. Apparently, it *wasn't* the time for jokes.

"Corona's in danger," said Rapunzel. "And it seems as if I'm the only one who wants to do anything about it!" She gazed out the window, where the morning sun covered Corona in a golden glow. It was hard to believe that just a

few miles away lay a threat that could destroy the entire kingdom.

Eugene joined Rapunzel at the window and took her hand. "You're *not* the only one," he said. "No matter what we're up against, Blondie, I'm with you all the way."

Rapunzel smiled at him. For all his jokes, Eugene was always there when she needed him, and she was grateful. "Thank you."

He gave her a hug. "I've got a feeling everything's going to be okay."

They were interrupted by shouting coming from the hallway. When they rushed out of the studio, they found Pete and Stan, two of the royal guards, arguing. Stan had tears in his eyes.

"All I said was your breath stinks," Pete was saying. "And you're a lousy croquet player. And your singing voice is awful!" Then he instantly slapped his hand over his mouth, horrified by how rude he had been.

Rapunzel stared at him in shock. "What are you doing? Stan's your best friend!"

"I know!" said Pete. "I can't help it! It's like I have to say whatever's on my mind!"

"Yeah, well . . ." Stan struggled to come up with an insult for Pete. "You . . . you have cookie crumbs on your cheek!"

Pete shrugged and brushed the purple crumbs off his face. That wasn't much of an insult, and Stan knew it. Frustrated, Stan gulped back a sob and ran off. Pete hurried after him. "Stan! Wait! I'm sorry!"

Eugene stopped Rapunzel from going after them. She had enough to worry about. "Get some rest," he told her. "I'll handle this."

Rapunzel nodded, grateful again for Eugene's support. Exhaustion had caught up with her, and a nap was exactly what she needed. Maybe her dreams would give her another clue—and she'd wake up knowing what she needed to do.

*R*apunzel was awakened by music coming from somewhere inside the castle. She got out of bed and followed the sound down the hallway to the royal ballroom. The doors swung open as if they'd been waiting for her to arrive.

Inside the ballroom, members of the court waltzed across the marble floor while an orchestra played. On the opposite side of the room stood King Frederic. "I feel horrible about the way we left things," he told Rapunzel, holding out his hands to her. "I want to make it up to you."

"I'm so relieved to hear that!" Rapunzel said,

running to take her father's hands.

They began to dance when suddenly, huge, spiky black rocks burst up through the floor between them. Within seconds, more rocks broke through the marble. They surrounded Rapunzel, rising above her head to the ceiling.

One of the rocks impaled Rapunzel's braid. She yanked her hair loose and ran to the door, her long hair flying out behind her.

Rocks filled the doorway, preventing her from leaving. Just then, Varian appeared behind her, clutching a thick strand of her hair. "Face your destiny," he told her in a menacing voice, a grim expression on his face. "Or all you hold in your heart will be in grave danger ..."

Rapunzel blinked awake. Her long hair swirled around her as Varian's words echoed in her

ears. A strand wrapped around Pascal, who was lying in his branch bed. Rapunzel's hair squeezed him tightly. Realizing what was happening, she burst out of bed and quickly freed her friend, who was quaking with fear. "You know I would *never* do anything to hurt you," she assured him. Pascal nodded and gave her a weak smile.

Rapunzel smiled in return, but she was still secretly afraid. *She* might not have meant to hurt him—but her hair seemed to have a mind of its own.

She placed Pascal gently on her shoulder. Her dream hadn't given her any answers—at least, not any she understood. Resting hadn't helped, but she knew what might. . . .

Rapunzel leaned over the side of the gondola

and dragged her fingers through the cool water of the lagoon surrounding the castle and its village. Then she sat and hugged her knees to her chest. Pascal perched quietly on her shoulder.

Rapunzel sometimes sailed around the

lagoon when she needed a place to think. The soft lapping of the water against the boat, the breeze against her face, and the deepness of the blue sky above helped her concentrate.

The water was calm and the breeze was still, but Rapunzel's thoughts remained a jumble of questions. Where had the black rocks come from? What did they want? Why did they always seem to be coming after *her*?

Suddenly, a small, dark figure leaped off a nearby dock and landed at Rapunzel's feet.

"Ruddiger!" cried Rapunzel, recognizing Varian's raccoon. "Where did you—"

A hand clamped over her mouth before she could finish. *"Shh!"* a voice hissed behind her. Rapunzel spun around to see Varian, who had also leaped onto the gondola.

Rapunzel immediately hugged her friend. "I've been so worried about you!" she said. "I'm very sorry about your father." She shivered at the memory of Quirin trapped in the amber. "I know now that's why you came for help during the storm."

Varian shrugged. "You had to save the kingdom. You did what you had to do." He explained how Quirin had become trapped after a potion Varian had concocted to dissolve the rocks had failed and had created the amber instead.

Rapunzel told him she'd found the scroll. "I have no idea what it is," she said as she handed it to him. "But my dad was desperate to keep it from me."

Varian unrolled the piece of paper. He'd discovered it in his father's trunk and realized it held important information about the rocks. "From what I can tell, the black rocks are some kind of ancient darkness," he said, pointing to the strange symbols. "The

61

destructive power of that darkness can only be stopped by the rocks' counterpart: the sundrop."

The sundrop was a magical flower that had grown from a single drop of sunlight. It had been found at the edge of a cliff outside Corona and boiled into a soup for Rapunzel's mother, Queen Arianna, after the queen had fallen ill while pregnant with Rapunzel. The flower's golden color and magical healing power had been reborn in Rapunzel's hair. The cliff where the flower was found was the *same* cliff where Rapunzel had first seen the black rocks.

"My dad said the flower was long gone," Rapunzel told Varian.

"And you believe him?"

Rapunzel thought about it. Her father had lied to her about the rocks. Who knew what

other lies he'd told her since she'd returned home?

"The sundrop is still in the castle," Varian insisted. "I'm sure of it. Your dad wouldn't throw away something that powerful." He rolled up the scroll and put it in his satchel. "A single petal could solve all of our problems."

Rapunzel knew he was right. They *had* to find the flower. But how? "Even if the flower *is* here, we can't just ask my dad to hand it over," she pointed out.

"I know." Varian grinned. "That's why we have to *steal* it."

Eugene peered into the mirrored breastplate of a suit of armor, squinting at his reflection.

Cassandra's face appeared over his shoulder. "It's hard to look away from shiny things, huh?" she said.

He ignored Cassandra's teasing tone. "The royal chef told me my ears were too big for my head." Eugene was fond of his ears—he'd had them all his life! It was upsetting to think they might be harming his overall handsomeness.

"No, your ears aren't too big," Cassandra insisted. Eugene smiled, relieved. "Your head's

just too small," she added with a chuckle.

"Seriously," he said, frowning. "People are acting really strange."

Cassandra had noticed that, too. While passing through the castle foyer earlier, she'd been startled by what she'd seen—or rather, *heard*.

Cassandra led Eugene to the foyer, which was crowded with servants and court members coming and going. There was nothing odd about that. The foyer was usually the busiest part of the castle. What *was* odd was what the servants and court members were saying.

"I dropped the king's éclair on the floor," the royal baker said as he passed by. "But I gave it to him anyway!"

"I stole half of these medals from the supply

cabinet!" declared a general, tapping the ribbons pinned to his uniform.

"I haven't taken a bath in five days!" exclaimed a guard.

No one seemed to be talking to anyone else. They just shouted their declarations, then clapped their hands over their mouths in embarrassment and ran off.

"This reminds me of Xavier's mood potion," Eugene told Cassandra. Xavier the blacksmith had invented the potion to reverse people's personalities. Pascal and Max had put a few drops in some lemonade—with nearly disastrous results. Happy people were suddenly sad. Calm people became instantly anxious. "Only now," Eugene continued, "everyone can't help but tell the truth."

"Out of my way, big ears!" barked a carriage driver, brushing past Eugene.

Eugene scowled. "Except that guy. He has *no idea* what he's talking about."

Cassandra rolled her eyes. Eugene needed to forget about his huge ears and focus on the problem. "If this *is* some kind of truth potion, we have to figure out how it got into the castle," she said. "Who was the first person you noticed being a little too honest?"

Eugene didn't have to think long. He told Cassandra how he'd chased down Pete and Stan after their fight. He had made Pete promise to be nicer to Stan, but Pete's words of apology hadn't sounded very sincere.

Now Eugene knew why. . . .

In another part of the castle, Rapunzel led Varian into the royal library.

"What are we doing *here*?" Varian demanded. "The flower's probably in the royal vault, and that's—"

"On the other side of the castle," Rapunzel said, interrupting him. "I know. But to get past the vault's security, we'll need to use the underground tunnels. Herz der Sonne's journal has a complete map of them." Herz der Sonne had been Corona's king centuries earlier and had built the tunnels during a war, as a way to move supplies in secret.

Varian followed Rapunzel to the rear of the library, where a large book sat open atop a pedestal. As Rapunzel picked up the book, she caught sight of King Frederic's portrait on the

library wall. His eyes seemed to stare down at her, disapproving.

"What am I doing?" she asked herself.

Varian noticed her hesitation. "This might be my dad's only hope," he told her. "It might be *Corona's* only hope."

Rapunzel was worried that taking the flower could be considered treason—something meant to harm the kingdom. But she wanted to *help* Corona. That *had* to make it okay.

At least, she hoped so.

As Rapunzel and Varian exited the library with the

book, they spotted Eugene at the opposite end of the hallway. Varian ducked behind a statue, out of sight.

"Hey, Blondie!" Eugene said. "Have you seen Pete?" He and Cassandra had split up to look for the guard.

"Nope." Rapunzel hid the journal behind her back. "Sorry." She felt Varian take the book from her hands and she let out a quiet sigh of relief.

Eugene sensed her nervousness. "Are you okay?" he asked.

Rapunzel tried to push away the guilt she still felt about Varian's plan. "How far would you go to find the truth?" she asked him.

This seemed to Eugene like an odd question to ask out of the blue, but he'd been thinking a

72

lot about the truth in the last few hours. He'd seen how hurtful it could be when people said whatever they thought—like telling somebody he had big ears, for instance. "Frankly, the truth's not all it's cracked up to be," he said.

This wasn't the answer Rapunzel had hoped to hear. Was Eugene trying to warn her? Had he figured out what she was up to?

Eugene noticed that her uneasiness had returned. "You *sure* you're all right?"

Rapunzel could tell from Eugene's concerned expression that he *didn't* know what she was up to. And she couldn't tell him. Not yet. He might try to stop her. "I've just had a lot to process lately," she said.

Eugene nodded. He trusted Rapunzel to tell him what was going on when she was ready.

He gave her a quick hug and headed off to continue his search for Pete.

Once Eugene was out of sight, Rapunzel signaled to Varian that it was safe to come out. As they made their way silently down the hall, she tried to leave her doubts behind. She was doing the right thing, she told herself again.

This time, she nearly believed it.

According to the sketches in Herz der Sonne's journal, the entrance to the tunnels lay a few feet beyond the stables. At first the spot seemed to be just a large patch of grass, but when Rapunzel and Varian looked closer, they found a rusted handle half-buried in the ground. They tugged on it, lifting a small trapdoor. Inside, a ladder led down into the darkness beyond.

Varian carried his lantern made of glowing compounds and went down first, followed by

Ruddiger, who had joined them. Rapunzel went last, with Pascal on her shoulder and the journal clutched under her arm.

The tunnels were wide, with high ceilings that absorbed the light from the lantern. Rapunzel had to squint to read the tunnel map. "This way," she said, pointing down a nearby path.

As they made their way through the passageway, Varian swung the lantern left and right, fascinated by the strange gears attached to the ceiling's wooden beams, and by the hinged metal plates and brick-sized silver rectangles dotting the stone floor. "Wow. These tunnels depict an ancient pre-Corona technology that— *AH!*"

The lantern beam had caught sight of a

skeleton lying against the wall. Pascal covered his eyes in horror. Ruddiger, terrified, ducked behind Rapunzel.

"We've got to be careful," Rapunzel told Varian. "These tunnels are lined with deadly booby traps." This warning was written clearly in the journal. Unfortunately, the map didn't show *where* the booby traps were.

"You may recall that I know a thing or two

about booby traps," replied Varian. Rapunzel nodded, remembering his glue trap.

Varian knew that unlike most of *his* traps, which were chemical, the traps in the tunnels were mechanical. That way, they'd never spoil or dry up and could last for years—until someone triggered them. He raised the lantern to take a closer look at the gears in the ceiling. It seemed likely they were part of one of these traps.

He didn't notice until too late that he'd stepped on the trigger—a silver brick in the floor. As his foot hit the brick, the gears turned, making a grinding, clunking sound. The walls on either side of them closed in. A second later, a wall dropped down in front of them, and another behind them.

They were trapped.

Varian and Rapunzel pushed on the moving walls but couldn't slow them down. "We're going to get squished!" shouted Varian.

Rapunzel spotted a small opening in the corner of the ceiling, where the wall with the gears met the wall in front of them.

"Can you get through there?" she asked Pascal, pointing to the hole. "If you can find the motor running this trap, you might be able to turn it off." She hated to put her little friend in danger—but if nothing was done, they'd *all* be crushed.

Pascal gathered his courage and darted up the wall. He slipped through the opening to the other side, where he discovered a rumbling machine with three levers. He raced

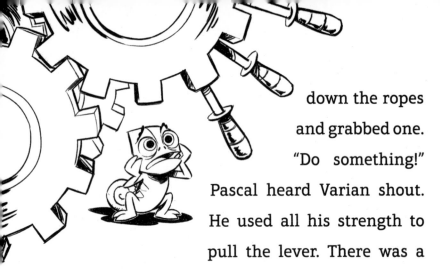

down the ropes and grabbed one. "Do something!" Pascal heard Varian shout. He used all his strength to pull the lever. There was a *clunk*. A second later, he heard the gears speed up. "That's the wrong something!" Varian screamed.

Inside the giant trap, the walls continued to close in on Rapunzel, Varian, and Ruddiger, until they could no longer move. Just when it seemed they'd be flattened, the walls stopped, the gears reversed, and finally, the walls moved apart. "You did it!" Rapunzel called to Pascal.

Varian doubled over, his face pale. "You might want to step aside," he gasped. "I think I'm going to be sick."

As the wall in front of them rose, Pascal dashed out. He scurried up to Rapunzel's shoulder, and she smiled at him with relief and gratitude.

Being caught and charged with treason for stealing the flower was no longer Rapunzel's greatest fear. Now she only hoped they could get through these tunnels alive. . . .

CHAPTER 5

Eugene and Cassandra's quest wasn't as dangerous as Rapunzel and Varian's, but it was proving to be almost as difficult. They had found Pete and brought him to the barracks behind the castle, where the royal guards slept. It was empty during the day, so they could question him without anyone interrupting.

Pete insisted he didn't know anything about a truth potion. But Cassandra was sure he knew more than he was saying—even if he didn't *know* he knew. "Start at the beginning," she told him. "Walk us through your day."

Pete, nervous, slumped down in his chair.

"Relax," said Eugene, putting a comforting hand on the guard's shoulder. "Just tell us what happened."

Pete thought back to that morning. "Well, I woke up confused because my mouth tasted like beans, but I had no memory of eating beans yesterday. Then I saw my cat and I said, 'Hello, Mr. Happy Paws!' And then he—"

"*Gah!*" exclaimed Cassandra. "All this information is useless!"

Pete shrank farther into his chair. "But you said—"

Eugene stepped in front of Cassandra. "Let's try this," he said to Pete. "Can you remember anything *out of the ordinary*?"

Pete thought a minute. "I thought the man

in the bush who gave me purple cookies was a
bit weird."

"You could have started with *that,*" snapped
Cassandra.

"Everybody's been eating them!" Pete said.

He forgot about being scared of Cassandra as he pictured the yummy cookies. "Talking about them makes me want another one!" He'd kept an extra in his pocket to have as a snack, and he drew it out now.

Cassandra slapped the cookie out of his hand. "Don't eat that!" she cried. "It could be laced with truth serum!"

She and Eugene exchanged a look as Pete stared down sadly at his crumbled cookie. It seemed pretty certain that they'd found the source of all the truth-telling going on around the castle.

Down in the tunnels, Rapunzel and Varian continued on their way, but they kept their eyes peeled for possible traps. Making sure to hold

their arms away from the walls, they stepped around the silver bricks and metal plates in the floor.

"Trip wire," Varian said, pointing ahead to a thread crossing their path at ankle height. He and Rapunzel stepped over the wire—but Ruddiger wasn't listening. He walked right into it, snapping it free from the wall and causing a hailstorm of boulders to rain down from the ceiling a few feet in front of them.

Luckily, no one was hurt. "We need to be more careful," Rapunzel warned the others. "We're getting closer to the vault. We don't want to alarm the guards."

Varian chuckled as they made their way around the rocks. "I'm pretty sure the guards have their hands full."

Rapunzel glanced over at Varian, confused by his odd comment. "What do you mean?" she asked.

"Nothing," Varian said quickly. "Just that they have their hands full every day! 'Corona! Busiest kingdom on earth!'" He leaned against the wall, trying to act casual—and triggered another trap. There was a loud rumble—and then the ground opened up behind them.

"Run!" cried Rapunzel. They bolted ahead as the ground continued to fall away.

Any second, they'd tumble into the abyss.

As she ran, Rapunzel glanced up at the beams in the ceiling. If only they had a rope, they could pull themselves up. . . .

But they *did* have a rope—or rather, something just as good! Rapunzel yanked the clasp from her braid, freeing her hair, then tossed her hair over one of the beams.

Varian quickly threw his arms around her, and Ruddiger latched onto Rapunzel's hair. Rapunzel swung them toward a glowing opening high in the wall as the rest of the ground below them gave way.

They landed inside the opening and paused to catch their breath. That had been a close call. *Too* close, Rapunzel felt. She hoped the flower was worth it. . . .

* * *

Out in the barracks, Eugene and Cassandra continued to grill Pete about the mysterious man with the cookies. "What else can you tell us about him?" asked Eugene.

"His voice was kind of squeaky," Pete replied. "And he asked about the sundrop."

"*The* sundrop?" Eugene asked, surprised. "Why would someone ask about something that's long gone?"

"It's *not* gone," said Pete. "The king's kept it hidden in the vault, ever since he used a petal from it to cure the queen." Pete slapped his hand over his mouth. The existence of the flower was a secret! Those cookies *were* dangerous . . . even if they were delicious.

Aha! thought Eugene. *That's what the guy with the truth serum was after—the flower.*

"So someone with a *squeaky voice* used a *potion* to get information about a *magical flower*," said Cassandra. She turned to Eugene. "Sound like anyone we know?"

Eugene nodded. *"Varian."*

If Pete had told Eugene and Cassandra the secret, he'd told Varian, too. Had Varian told Rapunzel? Was that why she'd been acting so strange when Eugene saw her in the hall?

"Rapunzel might be in trouble," said Eugene. "We need to get into the vault."

CHAPTER 6

The opening in the wall turned out to be part of another tunnel, and the glow Rapunzel had seen grew brighter as they headed down the passageway. The light seemed proof they were nearing the vault—and the flower.

The end of the tunnel opened into a round room with a high, domed ceiling. Pillars lined the walls, and a gigantic stone statue covered in rusty armor stood among them.

"We're under the vault," she said, pointing to a closed hatch in the ceiling.

"How do we get it open?" asked Varian.

Rapunzel counted the pillars. There were seven. A circular mosaic sat in the center of the floor, with seven short poles sticking up along its rim. The poles were probably levers— and one might open the hatch.

Or it could be another booby trap.

They'd come this far, though. They had to risk it.

Rapunzel grabbed one of the levers and pulled it toward herself. The mosaic spun around and the pillars lit up, sending off sparks. The door in the ceiling opened. It had worked!

Just then, they heard a loud creaking as the
giant statue broke free.

"Fascinating!" Varian exclaimed as the
statue lumbered toward them. "I believe it's an

automaton! A marvel of ancient technology. I've heard about them, but to see one in person is—"

"Look out!" Rapunzel shoved Varian out of the way as the statue swung its massive fist in their direction.

"Don't worry, Princess," Varian told her. "I've got this." He removed several tubes from his satchel and hurled them at the statue.

The tubes smashed against the automaton, dousing it in colorful liquids, but the mechanical monster didn't slow down. It scooped Varian up and flung him across the room, sending him crashing into the wall.

Rapunzel knew she had to do something— *quick*. She flung separate strands of her hair around two of the pillars and yanked. The pillars crashed down on top of the automaton, crushing it.

As Varian got to his feet, Rapunzel used her hair to pull the ladder from the ceiling inside the hatch. She and the others climbed up . . . and finally emerged at their destination: the vault.

On the far side of the room, a golden flower rested inside a teardrop-shaped vase dangling from a slender iron stand. Candlelight flickered behind a stained-glass image of the sun high in the wall, casting a warm glow on the delicate flower.

Rapunzel stared in awe. She'd heard stories about the sundrop and seen paintings of it, but to see it in person took her breath away. This was the flower that had given her hair its miraculous healing power! It was even *more* of a miracle that the flower was still alive.

Varian brushed past Rapunzel, startling her out of her daze. He snatched the flower from the vase and stuffed it into his satchel.

"You said you only needed one petal!" she protested.

"That might not be enough," replied Varian. "What difference does it make? It's just sitting here rotting."

Rapunzel grabbed the strap of Varian's satchel to retrieve the flower, and a thin, blue bottle fell out. She instantly recognized it. "That bottle had Xavier's mood potion in it!" she declared.

"There was only one drop left," Varian said as he picked up the bottle. "But it was enough for me to copy it." He grinned. "You'd be surprised what people will tell you for a cookie."

"How could you?" Rapunzel said in shock, thinking of Pete and Stan.

"Rapunzel, I used you." Varian shrugged. "I begged you and this kingdom for help, and everyone turned their back on me. It had to be this way."

Rapunzel was stunned. "I trusted you," she said. Looking at her friend in earnest, she continued, "Give me the flower, Varian. We can find a way to fix all this. I promise you. This isn't the way." She begged one last time. *"Please."*

Varian's eyes narrowed. "Sorry, Princess. But I know firsthand how well you keep promises."

Suddenly, the doors to the vault burst

open—and Eugene and Cassandra stormed in, along with Pete and two other guards. "Get him!" Eugene shouted, pointing to Varian.

Varian grabbed a tube from his satchel and smashed it to the floor. A cloud of smoke exploded in front of him.

When the smoke cleared, he was gone.

Later that night, Varian was hard at work in his lab. He dipped the tip of a drill into a paste he'd made by grinding a sundrop petal. If all went as planned, the sundrop's power would cause Quirin's crystal prison to shatter as soon as the paste hit the amber.

"Please work," Varian pleaded as he turned on the drill. He lowered the spinning drill bit to the amber, but the second it touched the

crystal, the bit exploded, sending shards of metal flying all around him.

"NO!" Varian hurled the drill across the room and dropped his face into his hands. "This is useless!" he sobbed. "It's as if the flower no longer holds the sundrop's power. . . ."

Varian lifted his head as his words sank in. He remembered testing Rapunzel's hair when she first came to his lab. Each test had proved it was unbreakable.

"The *sundrop* isn't the flower anymore," Varian murmured to himself. "It's *Rapunzel.* . . ."

CHAPTER 7

"The most important thing is your safety," King Frederic told Rapunzel in the throne room the next morning. He had just learned about Varian's theft of the sundrop.

Rapunzel was more concerned about the safety of the kingdom. "Varian's up to something, Dad," she said. "We need to—"

"*I'll* handle it, Rapunzel," the king said sternly. "Until Varian is no longer a threat, you will remain here, under guard, in the safest place in the castle."

Within the hour, Rapunzel and Pascal found themselves locked in their room high up in the tower, with two guards posted outside the door.

What the king seemed to have forgotten was that Rapunzel didn't need to get through the *door* to escape. "We're getting out of here," she told Pascal.

Using her long blond hair as a rope, she climbed down from her room's window. She'd sent Pascal ahead earlier, to deliver notes to Eugene and Cassandra detailing her plan.

Rapunzel's friends met her at the base of the tower, but just as they arrived, a dark fog surrounded the castle.

"The kingdom is being overcome by black rocks!" Varian shouted from somewhere within the fog. "The key to stopping them is Rapunzel!

I've asked for help and been ignored!" A huge claw emerged from the fog. "I will *not* be ignored any longer!"

King Frederic heard Varian's cries, and he dashed out of the castle, accompanied by several guards. "What are you doing out here?" he demanded when he saw Rapunzel. But before she could answer, the claw swept down and knocked the king's guards off their feet.

The claw belonged to a giant raccoon. Rapunzel realized that Varian had used one of his chemical formulas to turn Ruddiger into a monster.

More guards arrived, but their swords were useless against the beast. Luckily, Rapunzel had a better weapon. She lassoed her long hair around the creature and yanked him to the ground. A moment later, Ruddiger transformed back to his normal size.

As the tiny raccoon skittered away, another

guard raced out of the castle. "The queen is gone!" he cried.

Rapunzel felt a stab of fear. She realized the giant raccoon had been a diversion.

Varian had kidnapped her mother.

Rapunzel and her father hurried toward the king and queen's private quarters, but it was too late. The queen was really

gone. The king looked to his daughter, who had proved once again that she was more capable than he'd given her credit for. It was time to tell her the truth about the rocks.

"I'd been warned that taking the sundrop when your mother fell ill would awaken a darkness," the king told her. "I've known about the rocks all along, but I chose to ignore them because I didn't want to believe they were the result of my actions. But the truth is, the rocks *are* destroying Corona—and I'm responsible." The king bowed his head in shame. "It's all my fault."

"Mom's going to be okay," Rapunzel assured him. "We'll get her back." She took her father's hands. "And we'll find a way to save the kingdom—*together.*"

* * *

Rapunzel knew Varian would be expecting the king's forces to storm his house and rescue the queen. However, the attack could work as a diversion. While Varian was battling Corona's army, Rapunzel and the king could use Herz der Sonne's tunnels to sneak up *under* his house.

The captain of the guard had been too badly injured by the giant Ruddiger to lead the attack, but he designated a new leader: Cassandra. Eugene and his friend Lance joined Cassandra as she led the army to Old Corona. When they reached Varian's house, they quickly discovered that Rapunzel had been right—Varian *had* expected them to attack, and he'd created an army of automatons to fight back.

Meanwhile, Rapunzel, Pascal, and the king

made their way through the tunnels. They arrived beneath Varian's house, where a ladder led to a hatch in the ceiling. They climbed the ladder and entered Varian's lab to find that they'd stepped right into a glue trap.

Varian emerged from the shadows, grinning coldly. "Welcome back, Princess," he said. He quickly tied up Rapunzel and then the king, and locked Pascal in a small cage. After setting the cage on a high shelf, he drew back a curtain to reveal Queen Arianna, who was chained to the floor.

"Let her go," Rapunzel begged him. "Please."

"First you have to do something for me," replied Varian. "I need your hair to shatter the amber and free my father."

Varian grabbed a strand of Rapunzel's hair

and fed it into a funnel attached to the side of a drill four times the size of the drill he'd used earlier. Her hair passed through and threaded around the bit of the drill. When Varian turned the drill on, Rapunzel could feel her energy being drained. She squeezed her eyes, trying not to faint.

"No!" protested the king.

"It's my choice, Dad." Rapunzel nodded to Varian, who pressed the drill into the amber.

The bit made a screeching noise as it skidded over the surface of the amber, but it didn't break through.

Varian lowered the drill, confused. "I don't understand. . . ." He was too upset to notice Pascal tip the box he was trapped in off the shelf to the floor. The glass broke; then Pascal dashed

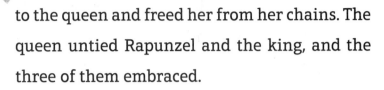

to the queen and freed her from her chains. The queen untied Rapunzel and the king, and the three of them embraced.

Rapunzel looked around for Varian, but he'd disappeared. She and her parents hurried outside, where Cassandra and her army were still battling dozens of Varian's automatons.

A new automaton stepped out from behind the house. "Sorry, Princess!" Varian yelled from inside the machine's giant head. "If I can't have a happy ending, neither can you!" His automaton snatched up Cassandra with one hand and the queen with the other.

Rapunzel knew there was only one way to defeat him. She had to use the rocks.

She grabbed hold of the two black spikes closest to her. As her hair glowed and swirled around her, a blinding light flashed from the rocks. The ground shook with a huge explosion as hundreds of new rocks sprang out of the earth, trapping Varian's automaton and shattering the others.

Cassandra and the queen stepped from the fallen automaton, unharmed. Guards quickly arrested Varian while Eugene hurried to Rapunzel, who had collapsed.

"We've got to find better ways to spend your birthdays," he said as he helped her to her feet. Rapunzel smiled, but when she gazed past Eugene, her eyes widened in shock.

The rocks had broken through the outer wall of the kingdom behind Varian's house. Strangely, they no longer pointed up. Instead, their pointy tops lay flat against the ground, forming a road that led out of Corona . . . to the kingdoms beyond.

"It's as if they want us to follow them," said Rapunzel.

The king and queen approached her. "I've

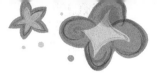

been afraid to let you go," the king said, taking her hand. "But the path is yours to follow."

The queen took Rapunzel's other hand. "Find your destiny, Rapunzel."

Rapunzel stared at the winding path the rocks had made. They were clearly leading her in one direction.

She still had so many questions about them, and about her connection to them. But it seemed as if the only way to find the answers was to follow the path. . . .

The End

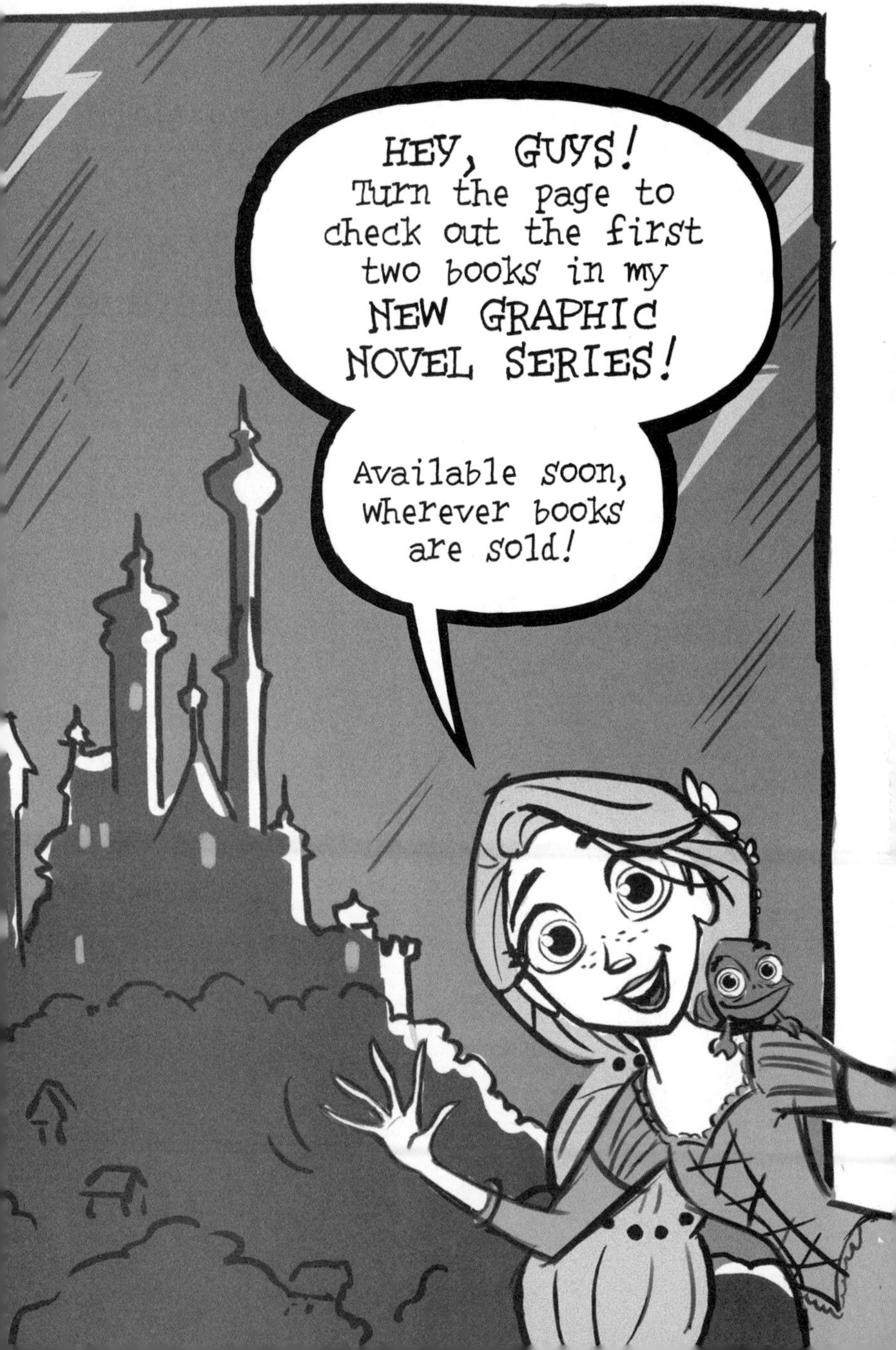
HEY, GUYS!
Turn the page to check out the first two books in my NEW GRAPHIC NOVEL SERIES!
Available soon, wherever books are sold!

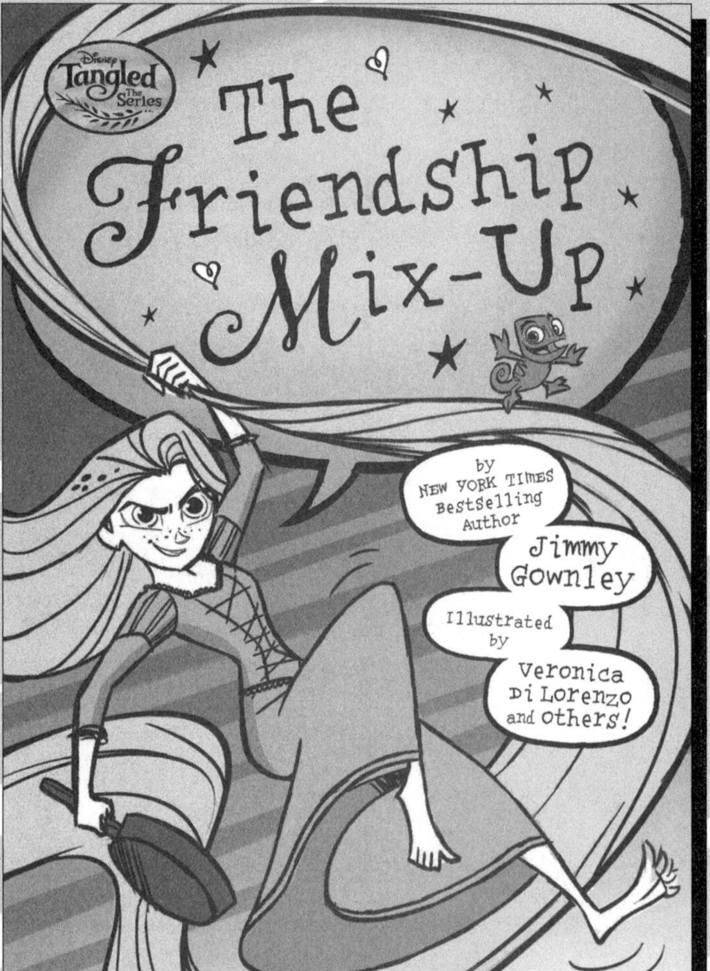
Disney Tangled The Series
The Friendship Mix-Up
by NEW YORK TIMES BestSelling Author
Jimmy Gownley
Illustrated by
Veronica Di Lorenzo and others!

Disney
Tangled
The Series
The Write Story
by
NEW YORK TIMES
Bestselling
Author
Jimmy
Gownley
Illustrated
by
Veronica
Di Lorenzo
and others!

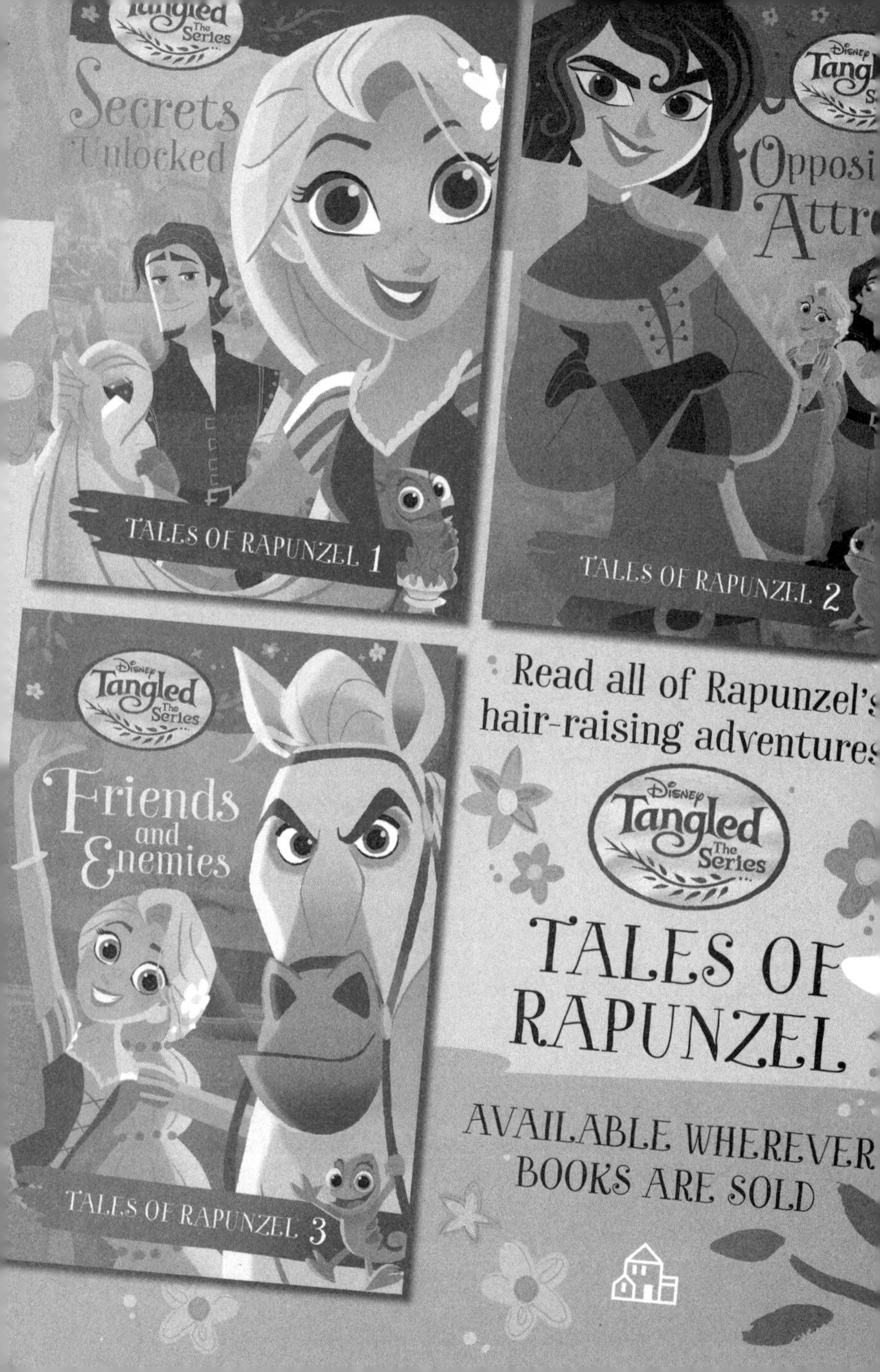
Secrets Unlocked
TALES OF RAPUNZEL 1
TALES OF RAPUNZEL 2
Disney Tangled The Series
Friends and Enemies
TALES OF RAPUNZEL 3
Read all of Rapunzel's
hair-raising adventures
Disney Tangled The Series
TALES OF RAPUNZEL
AVAILABLE WHEREVER
BOOKS ARE SOLD